Donated in memory of George Collins, father of Rev. John Collins.

From the Schadler Grandchildren

BY
MYSELF

BY MYSELF

by David Kherdian
pictures by Nonny Hogrogian

HENRY HOLT AND COMPANY • New York

Henry Holt and Company, Inc.
Publishers since 1866
115 West 18th Street
New York, New York 10011

Henry Holt is a registered
trademark of Henry Holt and Company, Inc.

Published in Canada by Fitzhenry & Whiteside Ltd.,
91 Granton Drive, Richmond Hill, Ontario L4B 2N5.

Library of Congress Cataloging-in-Publication Data
Kherdian, David.
By myself / by David Kherdian; pictures by Nonny Hogrogian.
Summary: A young girl on her way home from school talks
to all of her friends in the natural world around her, having
exchanges with trees, flowers, stones, and animals.
[1. Nature—Fiction.   2. Imagination—Fiction.]
I. Hogrogian, Nonny, ill.   II. Title.
PZ7.K527By   1993   [E]—dc20   92-44366

ISBN 0-8050-2386-0

First Edition—1993

Printed in the United States of America on acid-free paper. ∞

1   3   5   7   9   10   8   6   4   2

BY
MYSELF

I fell down in the school yard
and cut my knee.
When I tell my teacher, she says,
"It'll be all right," and sends me to the nurse.

The nurse puts something on it
that bubbles and makes it hurt.
Then she bandages it and says,
"I think you can go home now
and show it to your mother."

That's what I want to do,
so I say, "Thank you."
She walks me to the door and says,
"Good-bye. See you tomorrow."

I have never walked home from school before
that I can remember.
It is so quiet, so still.
There isn't anybody my size in the streets.
A dog comes along
and barks that he is happy to see me.
I tell him I am happy to see him, too.
His ears droop when he looks at my leg.
He says that he is sorry.
Then he runs up the street,
barking good-bye.

The birds are singing to each other.
They are singing about me.
I wave to them with my arms.
They wave back with their wings.
They fly over my head and all around me.
We are all together and dancing.
I skip and twirl and then I remember my knee
because it makes me remember.
It says ouch with my mouth
and I touch it smoothly and say I am sorry.
The birds understand and stop flying.
They look down from their branches at me.
I look up and say hello again.
They say hello and keep sitting.

Pretty soon the flowers start talking.
They talk to each other at first,
and then they talk to the butterflies and bees
and everything else that wants to be seen.
I stop and they talk to me.

I want to tell them what happened
but flowers don't keep secrets.
So I tell a stone that is looking at me.
"I wasn't pushed on purpose," I say.
The stone says he will keep my secret,
so I put him in my pocket.
The stone next to him overhears,
so I tell the stone that my friend shoved me,
but that he didn't mean to hurt me.
The stone says, "Of course he didn't,"
so I put this stone in my pocket, too.
Rocks don't always keep their secrets,
so I have to take them home.
I keep them with my other friends
in hidden places.
Only I can know where they are.

A squirrel chatters hello
and comes halfway down his tree,
his tail curved over his back.
   "I see you," the squirrel says.
"I see you with your secret stones."
   "And I see you with your secret nuts."
   "No you don't, no you don't."
   "Yes I do, yes I do."
   "No you don't, no you don't."
   "Well maybe I do," I say,
so the squirrel can win.
He runs back up the tree, satisfied.
He sits on his haunches,
pretending to eat a nut.

"He always does that," a stone says
that I hadn't noticed before.
"We know all his secrets.
Take me home, won't you?"
So I do, putting him in the other pocket
of my dress.

I will keep him in my busy box
under my bed,
for when the rain or thunder comes at night
and I can't fall back to sleep.

The trees are being very noisy and serious.
I look up at them and then at the sky.
I see why they are upset.
The sky is becoming gray
and seems to be in a very big hurry.
The sky is talking to a cloud,
but the cloud wants to get away.
And little by little it does.

"The wind is coming," the trees say at once.
"And then the rain."

   "Have I time to get home?" I ask the trees.

   "You are home," five maple trees in a row say,
their branches making a single crown that
sits softly atop their heads.

   "I know," I say. "But my mother doesn't
know this. And I must not get wet."
They say, "The rain is our friend,
but not always the wind."

   "It can't hurt you," I say,
"It only chases the things
that need to be chased."

"But it likes to get mad,
and it is always in a hurry."
  "It doesn't have much time," I say.
"And I don't, either.
Good-bye. See you tomorrow."
They are too busy
looking up at the sky to answer.
All at once the clouds are gone.
So is the old color of the sky.

The flowers turn away.
I feel a drop of rain on my cheek.
Soon it is talking to the ground,
and the ground is going everywhere at once,
unable to stop itself.
I run the rest of the way home
between the drops of rain.

Momma washes my knee
and puts a bandage on it.
The hurt is gone.
I go to my window seat
and watch the rain until it stops.

Now it is still,
and everything begins to change
back to the way it was.
But slowly.
All of my friends are talking at once:
trees, flowers, stones, animals;
and the cloud that went away
is starting to walk back across the sky.
Everything that was is itself again,
only different.

And I am different too,
sitting by myself,
looking out my window
after the rain comes down.

DEC 1 4 2011